牛
Ox

鼠
Rat

虎
Tiger

豬
PIg

兔
Rabbit

狗
Dog

龍
Dragon

For nearly 5,000 years, the Chinese culture has organized time in cycles of twelve years. This Eastern calendar is based upon the movement of the moon (as compared to the Western which follows the sun) and is symbolized by the zodiac circle. An animal that has unique qualities represents each year. Therefore, if you are born in a particular year, then you share the personality of that animal. Now people worldwide celebrate this two-week long festival in the early spring and enjoy the start of another Chinese New Year.

雞
Rooster

蛇
Snake

猴
Monkey

馬
Horse

羊
Sheep

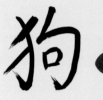

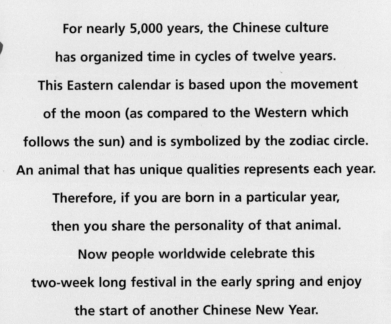

To my grandparents whose love and labor enabled
a better life for generations to come.
—O.C.

To my family—thank you for your love and support.
Without your selfless sacrifice, this book would not
have been possible. You truly are my greatest blessing.
—J.A.

immedium

Immedium, Inc.   P.O. Box 31846   San Francisco, CA 94131
www.immedium.com

Text Copyright ©2008 Oliver Chin
Illustrations Copyright ©2008 Jeremiah Alcorn

First hardcover edition published 2008.

Edited by Don Menn
Book design by Elaine Chu
Calligraphy by Lucy Chu

Printed in Singapore
10 9 8 7 6 5 4 3 2 1

Chin, Oliver Clyde, 1969-
  The year of the ox : tales from the Chinese zodiac / by Oliver Chin ;
illustrated by Miah Alcorn. -- 1st hardcover ed.
      p. cm.
  Summary: Olivia the ox learns what her best qualities really are when her
friend Mei needs help when a flood threatens their village. Lists the birth
years and characteristics of individuals born in the Chinese Year of the Ox.
  ISBN-13: 978-1-59702-015-2 (hardcover)
  ISBN-10: 1-59702-015-X
  [1. Oxen--Fiction. 2. Astrology, Chinese--Fiction.] I. Alcorn, Miah, ill. II.
Title.
  PZ7.C44235Ydr 2009
  [E]--dc22

2008003273
ISBN: 1-59702-015-X
ISBN 13: 978-1-59702-015-2

The Year of the Ox

·Tales from the Chinese Zodiac·

Written by Oliver Chin
Illustrated by Miah Alcorn

immedium
Immedium, Inc.
San Francisco

Light glistened off the morning dew, and the rising sun welcomed another day. Inside the stables, Mama and Papa Ox yawned after a long night. Resting in their bed of hay, they tickled their new baby.

Mama smiled,
"Hello there, honey."
Only a few hours
old, the youngster
was rustling
about already.

She had a sweet and
peaceful manner, so
Papa suggested,
"Let's call her Olivia."

The proud parents introduced the calf to their friends. "She'll be a big gal!" they all agreed.

Mama whispered, "Tomorrow you'll meet the farmer's daughter. Her name is Mei."

During her first visit, the girl petted Olivia and combed her hair. "I know we'll be best friends," smiled Mei, and she adopted Olivia as her little sister.

The grateful heifer promised, **"I'll always look out for you!"**

Sharing a bubbly spirit, the girls played
tag, "Hide and Seek," and "Kick the Can."
In the countryside, the pair loved to stop
and smell the roses. But sometimes their
wild wandering would make quite a mess.

Afterwards, Olivia's parents took her aside. Mama noted, "There's a time and place for fun and games."

Papa added, "Yes, dear — it's about time you learned to pull your own weight around here."

The following morning, Papa and Mama showed
her the shed where they got ready for work.
Every day the bull and cow would each carry
a yoke and pull a plow.

Olivia wanted to pitch in, despite Mama's misgivings. Papa pointed out, "But the yoke is heavy and tilling the ground is hard labor."

Olivia boasted, **"I'm a big girl now, and I can handle it by myself."**

But try as she might, Olivia was too small to plow the fields. Many times she got stuck in the mud and had to be rescued, **"Mooo!"**

After a long day, Olivia came home dirty and plum tuckered out.

After dinner Mama advised, "Dear, maybe you could try a different job."

"Yes, I'd like that very much," answered Olivia eagerly.

The next day, Mei led Olivia to the nearby well to fetch some water. Gingerly the girl filled her bucket and balanced it upon her head.

Her little sister bragged, **"Ha, I can carry much more than you!"**

"Be careful!" Mei warned as Olivia moseyed along with two buckets on her shoulders. They were almost home when a rooster bumped into them and crowed! Olivia slipped and spilled the water everywhere.

After cleaning up, Mei thought of another chore for Olivia: "Next week is harvest time. You could bring the rice to be milled." Olivia nodded, and they prepared to collect the crop.

During the harvest, Mei loaded stalks of grain onto Olivia's back.

"This is easy," smirked Olivia.

But on the way to the mill, a snake darted in front her. Startled, Olivia scattered her load all over the road!

Now both girls were embarrassed. But the weekend was here, and Mei's parents had planned to sell their vegetables at the local farmers market. Olivia promised to behave, so Mama and Papa let her come too.

The town square bustled with buying and selling, and Mei's parents displayed their bounty. Olivia marveled at all the sights, sounds, and smells. Meeting a friendly rat, she followed it to a stall close by.

Suddenly a yell rang out, "Eeeek!" Soon a crowd had gathered…to watch Olivia eat someone's fruit! Neighbors wagged their hooves, Papa shook his horns, and Mei hurried to drag her pal away.

After the commotion subsided, Mama moaned, "Darling, I guess you're not old enough to help us after all." Mei and her parents were disappointed too. So Olivia trudged back with her tail between her legs.

At home, Olivia wanted to prove she was a hard worker. But Mei's parents had business in town with Mama and Papa. Leaving to tend the fields, Mei told Olivia, "Please just stay behind and out of trouble."

Alone with little to do, Olivia vowed, **"I'll show them, somehow."**

Later she heard a cry pierce the sky, "Waaah!"

As noises suddenly filled the air, Olivia rushed outside and couldn't believe her eyes.

Everyone was running away from the farmland that was quickly flooding. The old dam had burst!

"Mooo!" bellowed Olivia, but no one stopped to help. Immediately she wondered, "Where is Mei?"

Olivia jumped into the rice paddy to search for her sister. Passersby warned her, "Leave while you can!"

But she pressed on against the current and finally spotted Mei clinging to the branches of a cypress tree.

Wet and worried, Mei was surprised to see Olivia, "What are you doing here?"

"This is no time for questions," Olivia sputtered.
"Get down and climb on board!"

Swimming towards home, Olivia picked up others stranded by the rising water. Juggling them on her shoulders, Olivia plowed ahead. At last, she clambered over the ridge to safety.

But before they could catch their breath, they noticed the bank had begun to buckle. If it gave way, the water would flood the village below.

Mei cried, "We need to warn the townsfolk!"

"Hurry up and go!" replied Olivia, as she pressed her shoulder against the dike. "I'll hold it up."

Hesitating, Mei hopped on her bicycle, "I'll pedal as fast as I can, and you'd better still be here when I come back!"

Leaning against the crumbling wall, Olivia spotted a crack where water began dripping through.

She needed to patch it, but didn't dare move. What could she do?

Hastily she stuck her tail into the hole!

PLUG!

The plug held, and Olivia sighed in relief. Feeling the world's weight on her shoulders, Olivia didn't want to let everybody down. Digging her hooves into the ground, she pushed with all her might.

"MoooOOo!!"

Time crawled by. Just then
Mei's family and Mama and Papa
arrived with lots of helpers.

As the waters finally receded,
Olivia took a break. She was
dirty, soggy, and hungry, but
was very happy.

Mei hugged Olivia, "Thanks for coming back for me."
Olivia blushed, **"I know you'd do the same."**

Joyfully Mama and Papa remarked,
"You two are the bravest
girls in the whole world."

Soon life returned to normal, and Olivia and Mei played their games and roamed about as before. Their parents watched how they were growing up, both hungry for adventure and strong-willed.

These sisters loved each other heart and soul. Mei knew that Olivia was there for her when it counted. And everyone around would remember that this was a marvelous Year of the Ox.

牛

Ox

1913, 1925, 1937, 1949, 1961, 1973, 1985, 1997, 2009, 2021

People born in the Year of the Ox are patient, stout, and down-to-earth. They are plain-spoken and hard-working. But sometimes they can be creatures of habit — cautious and headstrong. Though they may be slow to rouse, oxen are dependable characters indeed.